PROBLEM

PROBLEM

by Alan E. Nourse

The letter came down the slot too early that morning to be the regular mail run. Pete Greenwood eyed the New Philly photocancel with a dreadful premonition. The letter said:

PETER:
Can you come East chop-chop, urgent?
Grdznth problem getting to be a PRoblem, need expert icebox salesman to get gators out of hair fast.
Yes? Math boys hot on this, citizens not so hot.
Please come.
                    TOMMY

Pete tossed the letter down the gulper with a sigh. He had lost a bet to himself because it had come three days later than he expected, but it had come all the same, just as it always did when Tommy Heinz got himself into a hole.

Not that he didn't like Tommy. Tommy was a good PR-man, as PR-men go. He just didn't know his own depth. PRoblem in a beady Grdznth eye! What Tommy needed right now was a Bazooka Battalion, not a PR-man. Pete settled back in the Eastbound Rocketjet with a sigh of resignation.

He was just dozing off when the fat lady up the aisle let out a scream. A huge reptilian head had materialized out of nowhere and was hanging in air, peering about uncertainly. A scaly green body followed, four feet away, complete with long razor talons, heavy hind legs, and a whiplash tail with a needle at the end. For a moment the creature floated upside down, legs thrashing. Then the head and body joined, executed a horizontal pirouette, and settled gently to the floor like an eight-foot circus balloon.

Two rows down a small boy let out a muffled howl and tried to bury himself in his mother's coat collar. An indignant wail arose from the fat lady. Someone behind Pete groaned aloud and quickly retired behind a newspaper.

The creature coughed apologetically. "Terribly sorry," he said in a coarse rumble. "So difficult to control, you know. Terribly sorry...." His voice trailed off as he lumbered down the aisle toward the empty seat next to Pete.

The fat lady gasped, and an angry murmur ran up and down the cabin. "Sit down," Pete said to the creature. "Relax. Cheerful reception these days, eh?"

"You don't mind?" said the creature.

"Not at all." Pete tossed his briefcase on the floor. At a distance the huge beast had looked like a nightmare combination of large alligator and small tyrannosaurus. Now, at close range Pete could see that the "scales" were actually tiny wrinkles of satiny green fur. He knew, of course, that the Grdznth were mammals—"docile, peace-loving mammals," Tommy's PR-blasts had declared emphatically—but with one of them sitting about a foot away Pete had to fight down a wave of horror and revulsion.

The creature was most incredibly ugly. Great yellow pouches hung down below flat reptilian eyes, and a double row of long curved teeth glittered sharply. In spite of himself Pete gripped the seat as the Grdznth breathed at him wetly through damp nostrils.

"Misgauged?" said Pete.

The Grdznth nodded sadly. "It's horrible of me, but I just can't help it. I *always* misgauge. Last time it was the chancel of St. John's Cathedral. I nearly stampeded morning prayer—" He paused to catch his breath. "What an effort. The energy barrier, you know. Frightfully hard to make the jump." He broke off sharply, staring out the window. "Dear me! Are we going *east*?"

"I'm afraid so, friend."

"Oh, dear. I wanted *Florida*."

"Well, you seem to have drifted through into the wrong airplane," said Pete. "Why Florida?"

The Grdznth looked at him reproachfully. "The Wives, of course. The climate is so much better, and they mustn't be disturbed, you know."

"Of course," said Pete. "In their condition. I'd forgotten."

"And I'm told that things have been somewhat unpleasant in the East just now," said the Grdznth.

Pete thought of Tommy, red-faced and frantic, beating off hordes of indignant citizens. "So I hear," he said. "How many more of you are coming through?"

"Oh, not many, not many at all. Only the Wives—half a million or so—and their spouses, of course." The creature clicked his talons nervously. "We haven't much more time, you know. Only a few more weeks, a few months at the most. If we couldn't have stopped over here, I just don't know *what* we'd have done."

"Think nothing of it," said Pete indulgently. "It's been great having you."

The passengers within earshot stiffened, glaring at Pete. The fat lady was whispering indignantly to her seat companion. Junior had half emerged from his mother's collar; he was busy sticking out his tongue at the Grdznth.

The creature shifted uneasily. "Really, I think—perhaps Florida would be better."

"Going to try it again right now? Don't rush off," said Pete.

"Oh, I don't mean to rush. It's been lovely, but—" Already the Grdznth was beginning to fade out.

"Try four miles down and a thousand miles southeast," said Pete.

The creature gave him a toothy smile, nodded once, and grew more indistinct. In another five seconds the seat was quite empty. Pete leaned back, grinning to himself as the angry rumble rose around him like a wave. He was a Public Relations man to the core—but right now he was off duty. He chuckled to himself, and the passengers avoided him like the plague all the way to New Philly.

7

PROBLEM

But as he walked down the gangway to hail a cab, he wasn't smiling so much. He was wondering just how high Tommy was hanging him, this time.

*

The lobby of the Public Relations Bureau was swarming like an upturned anthill when Pete disembarked from the taxi. He could almost smell the desperate tension of the place. He fought his way past scurrying clerks and preoccupied poll-takers toward the executive elevators in the rear.

On the newly finished seventeenth floor, he found Tommy Heinz pacing the corridor like an expectant young father. Tommy had lost weight since Pete had last seen him. His ruddy face was paler, his hair thin and ragged as though chunks had been torn out from time to time. He saw Pete step off the elevator, and ran forward with open arms. "I thought you'd never get here!" he groaned. "When you didn't call, I was afraid you'd let me down."

"Me?" said Pete. "I'd never let down a pal."

The sarcasm didn't dent Tommy. He led Pete through the ante-room into the plush director's office, bouncing about excitedly, his words tumbling out like a waterfall. He looked as though one gentle shove might send him yodeling down Market Street in his underdrawers. "Hold it," said Pete. "Relax, I'm not going to leave for a while yet. Your girl screamed something about a senator as we came in. Did you hear her?"

Tommy gave a violent start. "Senator! Oh, dear." He flipped a desk switch. "What senator is that?"

"Senator Stokes," the girl said wearily. "He had an appointment. He's ready to have you fired."

"All I need now is a senator," Tommy said. "What does he want?"

"Guess," said the girl.

"Oh. That's what I was afraid of. Can you keep him there?"

8

"Don't worry about that," said the girl. "He's growing roots. They swept around him last night, and dusted him off this morning. His appointment was for *yesterday*, remember?"

"Remember! Of course I remember. Senator Stokes—something about a riot in Boston." He started to flip the switch, then added, "See if you can get Charlie down here with his giz."

He turned back to Pete with a frantic light in his eye. "Good old Pete. Just in time. Just. Eleventh-hour reprieve. Have a drink, have a cigar—do you want my job? It's yours. Just speak up."

"I fail to see," said Pete, "just why you had to drag me all the way from L.A. to have a cigar. I've got work to do."

"Selling movies, right?" said Tommy.

"Check."

"To people who don't want to buy them, right?"

"In a manner of speaking," said Pete testily.

"Exactly," said Tommy. "Considering some of the movies you've been selling, you should be able to sell anything to anybody, any time, at any price."

"Please. Movies are getting Better by the Day."

"Yes, I know. And the Grdznth are getting worse by the hour. They're coming through in battalions—a thousand a day! The more Grdznth come through, the more they act as though they own the place. Not nasty or anything—it's that infernal politeness that people hate most, I think. Can't get them mad, can't get them into a fight, but they do anything they please, and go anywhere they please, and if the people don't like it, the Grdznth just go right ahead anyway."

Pete pulled at his lip. "Any violence?"

Tommy gave him a long look. "So far we've kept it out of the papers, but there have been some incidents. Didn't hurt the Grdznth a bit—they have personal protective force fields around them, a little point they didn't bother to tell us about. Anybody who tries anything fancy gets thrown like a bolt of lightning hit him. Rumors are getting wild—people saying they can't be killed, that they're just moving in to stay."

Pete nodded slowly. "Are they?"

"I wish I knew. I mean, for sure. The psych-docs say no. The Grdznth agreed to leave at a specified time, and something in their cultural background makes them stick strictly to their agreements. But that's just what the psych-docs think, and they've been known to be wrong."

"And the appointed time?"

Tommy spread his hands helplessly. "If we knew, you'd still be in L.A. Roughly six months and four days, plus or minus a month for the time differential. That's strictly tentative, according to the math boys. It's a parallel universe, one of several thousand already explored, according to the Grdznth scientists working with Charlie Karns. Most of the parallels are analogous, and we happen to be analogous to the Grdznth, a point we've omitted from our PR-blasts. They have an eight-planet system around a hot sun, and it's going to get lots hotter any day now."

Pete's eyes widened. "Nova?"

"Apparently. Nobody knows how they predicted it, but they did. Spotted it coming several years ago, so they've been romping through parallel after parallel trying to find one they can migrate to. They found one, sort of a desperation choice. It's cold and arid and full of impassable mountain chains. With an uphill fight they can make it support a fraction of their population."

Tommy shook his head helplessly. "They picked a very sensible system for getting a good strong Grdznth population on the new parallel as fast as possible. The males were picked for brains, education, ability and adaptability; the females were chosen largely according to how pregnant they were."

Pete grinned. "Grdznth in utero. There's something poetic about it."

"Just one hitch," said Tommy. "The girls can't gestate in that climate, at least not until they've been there long enough to get their glands adjusted. Seems we have just the right climate here for gestating Grdznth, even better than at home. So they came begging for permission to stop here, on the way through, to rest and parturiate."

"So Earth becomes a glorified incubator." Pete got to his feet thoughtfully. "This is all very touching," he said, "but it just doesn't wash. If the Grdznth are so unpopular with the masses, why did we let them in here in the first place?" He looked narrowly at Tommy. "To be very blunt, what's the parking fee?"

"Plenty," said Tommy heavily. "That's the trouble, you see. The fee is so high, Earth just can't afford to lose it. Charlie Karns'll tell you why."

*

Charlie Karns from Math Section was an intense skeleton of a man with a long jaw and a long white coat drooping over his shoulders like a shroud. In his arms he clutched a small black box.

"It's the parallel universe business, of course," he said to Pete, with Tommy beaming over his shoulder. "The Grdznth can cross through. They've been able to do it for a long time. According to our figuring, this must involve complete control of mass, space and dimension, all three. And time comes into one of the three—we aren't sure which."

The mathematician set the black box on the desk top and released the lid. Like a jack-in-the-box, two small white plastic spheres popped out and began chasing each other about in the air six inches above the box. Presently a third sphere rose up from the box and joined the fun.

Pete watched it with his jaw sagging until his head began to spin. "No wires?"

"*Strictly* no wires," said Charlie glumly. "No nothing." He closed the box with a click. "This is one of their children's toys, and

PROBLEM

theoretically, it can't work. Among other things, it takes null-gravity to operate."

Pete sat down, rubbing his chin. "Yes," he said. "I'm beginning to see. They're teaching you this?"

Tommy said, "They're trying to. He's been working for weeks with their top mathematicians, him and a dozen others. How many computers have you burned out, Charlie?"

"Four. There's a differential factor, and we can't spot it. They have the equations, all right. It's a matter of translating them into constants that make sense. But we haven't cracked the differential."

"And if you do, then what?"

Charlie took a deep breath. "We'll have inter-dimensional control, a practical, utilizable transmatter. We'll have null-gravity, which means the greatest advance in power utilization since fire was discovered. It might give us the opening to a concept of time travel that makes some kind of sense. And power! If there's an energy differential of any magnitude—" He shook his head sadly.

"We'll also know the time-differential," said Tommy hopefully, "and how long the Grdznth gestation period will be."

"It's a fair exchange," said Charlie. "We keep them until the girls have their babies. They teach us the ABC's of space, mass and dimension."

Pete nodded. "That is, if you can make the people put up with them for another six months or so."

Tommy sighed. "In a word—yes. So far we've gotten nowhere at a thousand miles an hour."

*

"I can't do it!" the cosmetician wailed, hurling himself down on a chair and burying his face in his hands. "I've failed. Failed!"

The Grdznth sitting on the stool looked regretfully from the cosmetician to the Public Relations men. "I say—I *am* sorry...." His coarse voice trailed off as he peeled a long strip of cake makeup off his satiny green face.

Pete Greenwood stared at the cosmetician sobbing in the chair. "What's eating *him*?"

"Professional pride," said Tommy. "He can take twenty years off the face of any woman in Hollywood. But he's not getting to first base with Gorgeous over there. This is only one thing we've tried," he added as they moved on down the corridor. "You should see the field reports. We've tried selling the advances Earth will have, the wealth, the power. No dice. The man on the street reads our PR-blasts, and then looks up to see one of the nasty things staring over his shoulder at the newspaper."

"So you can't make them beautiful," said Pete. "Can't you make them cute?"

"With those teeth? Those eyes? Ugh."

"How about the 'jolly company' approach?"

"Tried it. There's nothing jolly about them. They pop out of nowhere, anywhere. In church, in bedrooms, in rush-hour traffic through Lincoln Tunnel—look!"

Pete peered out the window at the traffic jam below. Cars were snarled up for blocks on either side of the intersection. A squad of traffic cops were converging angrily on the center of the mess, where a stream of green reptilian figures seemed to be popping out of the street and lumbering through the jammed autos like General Sherman tanks.

"Ulcers," said Tommy. "City traffic isn't enough of a mess as it is. And they don't *do* anything about it. They apologize profusely, but they keep coming through." The two started on for the office. "Things are getting to the breaking point. The people are wearing thin from sheer annoyance—to say nothing of the nightmares the kids are having, and the trouble with women fainting."

The signal light on Tommy's desk was flashing scarlet. He dropped into a chair with a sigh and flipped a switch. "Okay, what is it now?"

PROBLEM

"Just another senator," said a furious male voice. "Mr. Heinz, my arthritis is beginning to win this fight. Are you going to see me now, or aren't you?"

"Yes, yes, come right in!" Tommy turned white. "Senator Stokes," he muttered. "I'd completely forgotten—"

The senator didn't seem to like being forgotten. He walked into the office, looked disdainfully at the PR-men, and sank to the edge of a chair, leaning on his umbrella.

"You have just lost your job," he said to Tommy, with an icy edge to his voice. "You may not have heard about it yet, but you can take my word for it. I personally will be delighted to make the necessary arrangements, but I doubt if I'll need to. There are at least a hundred senators in Washington who are ready to press for your dismissal, Mr. Heinz—and there's been some off-the-record talk about a lynching. Nothing official, of course."

"Senator—"

"Senator be hanged! We want somebody in this office who can manage to *do* something."

"Do something! You think I'm a magician? I can just make them vanish? What do you want me to do?"

The senator raised his eyebrows. "You needn't shout, Mr. Heinz. I'm not the least interested in *what* you do. My interest is focused completely on a collection of five thousand letters, telegrams, and visiphone calls I've received in the past three days alone. My constituents, Mr. Heinz, are making themselves clear. If the Grdznth do not go, I go."

"That would never do, of course," murmured Pete.

The senator gave Pete a cold, clinical look. "Who is this person?" he asked Tommy.

"An assistant on the job," Tommy said quickly. "A very excellent PR-man."

The senator sniffed audibly. "Full of ideas, no doubt."

14

"Brimming," said Pete. "Enough ideas to get your constituents off your neck for a while, at least."

"Indeed."

"Indeed," said Pete. "Tommy, how fast can you get a PR-blast to penetrate? How much medium do you control?"

"Plenty," Tommy gulped.

"And how fast can you sample response and analyze it?"

"We can have prelims six hours after the PR-blast. Pete, if you have an idea, tell us!"

Pete stood up, facing the senator. "Everything else has been tried, but it seems to me one important factor has been missed. One that will take your constituents by the ears." He looked at Tommy pityingly. "You've tried to make them lovable, but they aren't lovable. They aren't even passably attractive. There's one thing they *are* though, at least half of them."

Tommy's jaw sagged. "Pregnant," he said.

"Now see here," said the senator. "If you're trying to make a fool out of me to my face—"

"Sit down and shut up," said Pete. "If there's one thing the man in the street reveres, my friend, it's motherhood. We've got several hundred thousand pregnant Grdznth just waiting for all the little Grdznth to arrive, and nobody's given them a side glance." He turned to Tommy. "Get some copywriters down here. Get a Grdznth obstetrician or two. We're going to put together a PR-blast that will twang the people's heart-strings like a billion harps."

The color was back in Tommy's cheeks, and the senator was forgotten as a dozen intercom switches began snapping. "We'll need TV hookups, and plenty of newscast space," he said eagerly. "Maybe a few photographs—do you suppose maybe *baby* Grdznth are lovable?"

"They probably look like salamanders," said Pete. "But tell the people anything you want. If we're going to get across the sanctity of Grdznth motherhood, my friend, anything goes."

"It's genius," chortled Tommy. "Sheer genius."

PROBLEM

"If it sells," the senator added, dubiously.

"It'll sell," Pete said. "The question is: for how long?"

*

The planning revealed the mark of genius. Nothing sudden, harsh, or crude—but slowly, in a radio comment here or a newspaper story there, the emphasis began to shift from Grdznth in general to Grdznth as mothers. A Rutgers professor found his TV discussion on "Motherhood as an Experience" suddenly shifted from 6:30 Monday evening to 10:30 Saturday night. Copy rolled by the ream from Tommy's office, refined copy, hypersensitively edited copy, finding its way into the light of day through devious channels.

Three days later a Grdznth miscarriage threatened, and was averted. It was only a page 4 item, but it was a beginning.

Determined movements to expel the Grdznth faltered, trembled with indecision. The Grdznth were ugly, they frightened little children, they *were* a trifle overbearing in their insufferable stubborn politeness—but in a civilized world you just couldn't turn expectant mothers out in the rain.

Not even expectant Grdznth mothers.

By the second week the blast was going at full tilt.

In the Public Relations Bureau building, machines worked on into the night. As questionnaires came back, spot candid films and street-corner interview tapes ran through the projectors on a twenty-four-hour schedule. Tommy Heinz grew thinner and thinner, while Pete nursed sharp post-prandial stomach pains.

"Why don't people *respond?*" Tommy asked plaintively on the morning the third week started. "Haven't they got any feelings? The blast is washing over them like a wave and there they sit!" He punched the private wire to Analysis for the fourth time that morning. He got a man with a hag-ridden look in his eye. "How soon?"

"You want yesterday's rushes?"

"What do you think I want? Any sign of a lag?"

"Not a hint. Last night's panel drew like a magnet. The D-Date tag you suggested has them by the nose."

"How about the President's talk?"

The man from Analysis grinned. "He should be campaigning."

Tommy mopped his forehead with his shirtsleeve. "Okay. Now listen: we need a special run on all response data we have for tolerance levels. Got that? How soon can we have it?"

Analysis shook his head. "We could only make a guess with the data so far."

"Fine," said Tommy. "Make a guess."

"Give us three hours," said Analysis.

"You've got thirty minutes. Get going."

Turning back to Pete, Tommy rubbed his hands eagerly. "It's starting to sell, boy. I don't know how strong or how good, but it's starting to sell! With the tolerance levels to tell us how long we can expect this program to quiet things down, we can give Charlie a deadline to crack his differential factor, or it's the ax for Charlie." He chuckled to himself, and paced the room in an overflow of nervous energy. "I can see it now. Open shafts instead of elevators. A quick hop to Honolulu for an afternoon on the beach, and back in time for supper. A hundred miles to the gallon for the Sunday driver. When people begin *seeing* what the Grdznth are giving us, they'll welcome them with open arms."

"Hmmm," said Pete.

"Well, why won't they? The people just didn't trust us, that was all. What does the man in the street know about transmatters? Nothing. But give him one, and then try to take it away."

"Sure, sure," said Pete. "It sounds great. Just a little bit *too* great."

Tommy blinked at him. "Too great? Are you crazy?"

"Not crazy. Just getting nervous." Pete jammed his hands into his pockets. "Do you realize where *we're* standing in this thing? We're out on a limb—way out. We're fighting for time—time for Charlie and his gang to crack the puzzle, time for the Grdznth girls to gestate. But what are we hearing from Charlie?"

"Pete, Charlie can't just—"

"That's right," said Pete. "*Nothing* is what we're hearing from Charlie. We've got no transmatter, no null-G, no power, nothing except a whole lot of Grdznth and more coming through just as fast as they can. I'm beginning to wonder what the Grdznth *are* giving us."

"Well, they can't gestate forever."

"Maybe not, but I still have a burning desire to talk to Charlie. Something tells me they're going to be gestating a little too long."

They put through the call, but Charlie wasn't answering. "Sorry," the operator said. "Nobody's gotten through there for three days."

"Three days?" cried Tommy. "What's wrong? Is he dead?"

"Couldn't be. They burned out two more machines yesterday," said the operator. "Killed the switchboard for twenty minutes."

"Get him on the wire," Tommy said. "That's orders."

"Yes, sir. But first they want you in Analysis."

Analysis was a shambles. Paper and tape piled knee-deep on the floor. The machines clattered wildly, coughing out reams of paper to be gulped up by other machines. In a corner office they found the Analysis man, pale but jubilant.

"The Program," Tommy said. "How's it going?"

"You can count on the people staying happy for at least another five months." Analysis hesitated an instant. "If they see some baby Grdznth at the end of it all."

There was dead silence in the room. "Baby Grdznth," Tommy said finally.

"That's what I said. That's what the people are buying. That's what they'd better get."

Tommy swallowed hard. "And if it happens to be six months?"

Analysis drew a finger across his throat.

18

Tommy and Pete looked at each other, and Tommy's hands were shaking. "I think," he said, "we'd better find Charlie Karns right now."

*

Math Section was like a tomb. The machines were silent. In the office at the end of the room they found an unshaven Charlie gulping a cup of coffee with a very smug-looking Grdznth. The coffee pot was floating gently about six feet above the desk. So were the Grdznth and Charlie.

"Charlie!" Tommy howled. "We've been trying to get you for hours! The operator—"

"I know, I know." Charlie waved a hand disjointedly. "I told her to go away. I told the rest of the crew to go away, too."

"Then you cracked the differential?"

Charlie tipped an imaginary hat toward the Grdznth. "Spike cracked it," he said. "Spike is a sort of Grdznth genius." He tossed the coffee cup over his shoulder and it ricochetted in graceful slow motion against the far wall. "Now why don't you go away, too?"

Tommy turned purple. "We've got five months," he said hoarsely. "Do you hear me? If they aren't going to have their babies in five months, we're dead men."

Charlie chuckled. "Five months, he says. We figured the babies to come in about three months—right, Spike? Not that it'll make much difference to us." Charlie sank slowly down to the desk. He wasn't laughing any more. "We're never going to see any Grdznth babies. It's going to be a little too cold for that. The energy factor," he mumbled. "Nobody thought of that except in passing. Should have, though, long ago. Two completely independent universes, obviously two energy systems. Incompatible. We were dealing with mass, space and dimension—but the energy differential was the important one."

"What about the energy?"

"We're loaded with it. Super-charged. Packed to the breaking point and way beyond." Charlie scribbled frantically on the desk pad.

19

PROBLEM

"Look, it took energy for them to come through—immense quantities of energy. Every one that came through upset the balance, distorted our whole energy pattern. And they knew from the start that the differential was all on their side—a million of them unbalances four billion of us. All they needed to overload us completely was time for enough crossings."

"And we gave it to them." Pete sat down slowly, his face green. "Like a rubber ball with a dent in the side. Push in one side, the other side pops out. And we're the other side. When?"

"Any day now. Maybe any minute." Charlie spread his hands helplessly. "Oh, it won't be bad at all. Spike here was telling me. Mean temperature in only 39 below zero, lots of good clean snow, thousands of nice jagged mountain peaks. A lovely place, really. Just a little too cold for Grdznth. They thought Earth was much nicer."

"For them," whispered Tommy.

"For them," Charlie said.

www.ingramcontent.com/pod-product-compliance
Lightning Source LLC
Chambersburg PA
CBHW020144150626
46552CB00021B/1703